I0829402

For Aszure and Ohana.
Stay weird, stay wild,
and always take flight!

1
2
3
4
5
6
7
8
9
10
TEN
BALLOONS
Tiffani Joy Patterson

We are throwing a party.
HOORAY
HOORAY!

But what is a party
without balloons to play?

A party needs balloons.
That is just how it goes.
Then, woosh!
A red balloon drifts
past my nose.

One balloon twirling high,
dancing in the sky.

Then a blue balloon bounces in with flair.

Two balloons
now floating
through
the air.

Where did they
come from?
Nobody knows.
Maybe they followed the
scent of cake and bows.

Look up! Look there!
A third balloon arrives.
Three balloons swirl
like bees in a hive.
Did they bring friends?
Let us open the door.

In floats a bright one,
and now there
are four!

Four balloons bobbing,
full of cheer.
In glides a green one.
Now five are here!

Balloons galore,
colors bright.
This party is
pure delight!

Are there six? Let us count and see.
ONE
TWO
THREE

FIVE
FOUR
Yippee!
Yes!
Six balloons float
high and low,
waving hello
wherever they go.

Seven balloons now bounce and sway.
They giggle and wiggle all through the day.

What about eight?
Can we find more?
With a

**KNOCK,
KNOCK,
KNOCK,**

they burst
through the door!

Eight balloons shimmer,
shiny and bright.

Nine dance in with twinkling light.
Balloons spining, dipping, floating free.
A rainbow parade for all to see.

But wait! We are
missing just one friend.
Without ten, this party
might end.

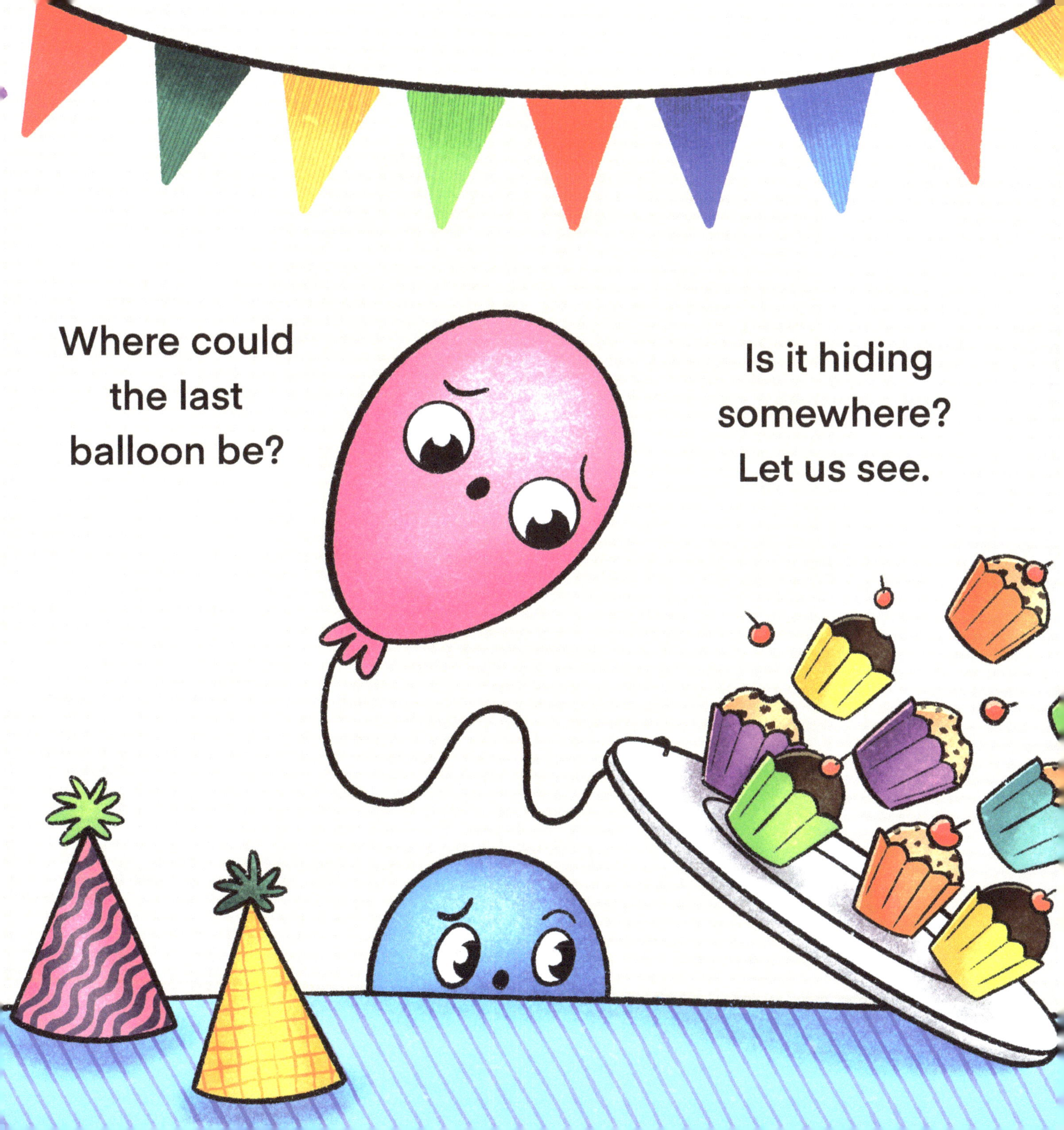

Where could the last balloon be?
Is it hiding somewhere? Let us see.

A golden balloon
comes floating
down, sparkling
like a royal crown.

Ten balloons at our party
at last! Time for cake...
....and big
birthday
blast!

With ten balloons and friends galore,
this is the party we have waited for!

Laughter, dancing, cake and fun.
A perfect party
for everyone!